HANDLE
WITH
CARE

EMILY PORTERFIELD

PIQUIN PRESS

CONTENTS

DEDICATION

To Herbert:
the echo of innocence past,
of kindred souls alight,
traversing the hourglass,
dreams aflight
a vapor,
a wrinkle in time
yes...
I will always remember

ACKNOWLEDGEMENTS

To my wonderful team who helped me make this book a reality. From my creative partners who assisted me in fleshing out this story; to my editors, Andrea and Tara, who pulled the best out of me; and finally to my most awesome cover designer, Damon - your talent continues to amaze me. I am deeply appreciative to all of you.

"Reflect upon your
present blessings,
of which every man has
many –
not on your past
misfortunes,
of which all men have
some."
~ Charles Dickens

» Chapter 1 «
~MIST~

Morning wasn't her favorite time. But no time was. It began with little fanfare, little fervor. Abby liked it that way. The stillness beckoned her to come out and simply be. She could merge into the unfolding scene with little expectation. It was quiet on the docks – a place to gather her thoughts, or not to have any. A slight chill in the air caused her to shudder, then pull her russet colored shawl a little more tightly around her shoulders. There she stood, staring into seeming nothingness, alone in the silence.

The water lapped effortlessly against the sides of the boat, its sound hypnotic and soothing. It reached into the tortured recesses of Abby's mind, seeking to offer her some semblance of peace. She stared across the water, embracing the stillness. Abby was fascinated by the morning fog, and how it obliterated any delineation between water and expansive sky. This was Oregon. Its endless beauty and intense natural forces were raw, primal, untainted. Her Uncle Patrick had been right - it was the most beautiful place she had ever seen. Yet, its splendor did nothing to kindle joy in her. The rugged scene inspired a sense of loneliness, hopelessness, emptiness, smallness... as if she were the horizon, lost in fog.

"Nice morning, hm?" The greeting came from a few steps behind her. Abby cringed and gritted her teeth. She didn't answer; she didn't want to be bothered. There was no energy to spare for discourse, nor interest. *Maybe he'll go away?*

Abby did not turn around, or in any way acknowledge she had heard him. The last thing she wanted was to face another human being, to deal with their expectations or judgments. Oh no... she just wanted him to go away.

"Ah, ma'am?" Reluctantly, she turned to face the man behind her. Her cinnamon eyes narrowed, clearly sending the message she had no desire for conversation.

"Yes," she replied in a cracked, annoyed voice. Clearing her dry throat, her mind wandered briefly. *What did I drink this morning?* In the past few days, since arriving in Winchester Bay, she had not said a word to anyone. She had pretty much stayed on her uncle's boat, dejected. And that was the point – isolation, seclusion, rest, not discussing the weather with a local fisherman. She didn't want to be bothered.

"We don't get too many newcomers around here," his tone was warm and amiable. "My name's Craig, and you are...?" Abby wasn't looking for friends, so his reception was undeniably cool. As his gaze swept over her, he couldn't help but notice the indifference; as though he were a ghost, his presence barely registering. He held out his hand, anyway.

"Craig Port, Ma'am," a more formal attempt. "Pleased to meet you."

Abby's lips twitched into an annoyed grimace as politeness forced her to take his hand. When she shook it, she noticed his skin was rough; enough calluses to show he spent time working. A long-sleeved flannel shirt, with frayed edges, covered his athletic frame. The jeans he wore had a few holes, too. His leather boots were scuffed with a bit of dried mud defiantly clinging to the rubber sole. The brim of his cap was pulled down low over his forehead, darkening his green eyes in shadow. Above square lips framed with smile lines, the curves of his bristled cheeks were flushed crimson from being outdoors. Only the curls of his brown hair were at odds with his relaxed demeanor; they did not seem the slightest bit out of place.

"Abigail Miles," she offered in return. "I'm just visiting for a little while," she added, hoping this would dispel his interest.

"With family?" Craig prompted, attempting to continue the dialog. Abby felt uneasy with his question. He was overstepping the line of friendly curiosity into being nosy.

"No, no... my uncle... his boat," she said in a hurried, dismissive fashion, not wanting to reveal anything. "I really should be going." Abby started to walk past him along the dock, brushing his arm as she maneuvered by in the narrow space.

"Well, I hope you enjoy your stay," he called out. Craig didn't try to hide his harsh tone; there was no need for her to brush him off.

Abby did not reply as she stepped off of the dock and onto her uncle's houseboat, beating a hasty retreat. Craig watched her with a mixture of curiosity and unease. There was something about her that did not feel right. In a town of less than six hundred people, it was easy to notice a stranger. It was easier still to peg someone who did not fit in the Winchester Bay lifestyle. He shook his head and continued along the dock to his small fishing boat. After all, it was Saturday - his day to enjoy the open water. A few hours away from his responsibilities, and Abby wasn't his concern.

* * *

Abby emphatically closed the door behind her. She did not want to make any friends, none whatsoever. She wanted to be left alone, to remain anonymous, and "enjoy" time away from the chaos she left behind... chaos she felt entirely responsible for. She wanted to lose herself in silence.

As she stretched out across the bunk, she wondered, for the thousandth time, how she had ended up here. Once she had been a prominent psychologist, specializing in working with traumatized war veterans from the conflicts in Iraq and Afghanistan. Abby was praised highly for her ability to reach the most broken men and women who were returning from incredibly harrowing experiences. She closed her eyes against the flood of patient faces through her memory. The vain pride she once had in herself was gone. The pain rose within her – the self-loathing and intense need to escape – it was enough to make her wish she could disappear. That was why she was here. To disappear. Sadly, it would take more than Winchester Bay's soothing qualities to rescue a woman as lost as Abby.

* * *

The next morning, when she awakened, Abby could not immediately recall where she was. The sunlight battled its way through the gritty window and splintered across the white wall of the small bedroom. Abby sighed as the real world unwound around her. Ready or not, she was being forced to face it. She always treasured those few seconds just before opening her eyes; a few blissful moments in which she was simply Abby, again. Although she had compassion for her patients, she had never truly understood the depths of their despair, their inability to release, to move on from a trauma. Now she did. Now she saw her arrogance with such painful clarity - it wounded her.

I can't believe I used to say, "Let's keep focusing on the positive," or "Time heals all wounds." How utterly trite! Abby groaned. *Stupid, stupid, stupid.* She struck the pillow with her fists repeatedly, burying her face in it. Sitting up, she grabbed each end of the pillow and yanked it, this way and that, in a frenzied crescendo of fury. *Arrrghhh!* With the pillow still clenched in her hands, she plunged her face into it again, screaming her pain and frustration into its billowy softness - the down inside muffling the tortured sound. Her fit of anguish spent, Abby pulled the pillow down from her red, puffy face, hugging it as she rocked back and forth, sobbing softly. A river of tears flowed down her cheeks.

Her stomach rumbled, distracting her momentarily from her grief. *When was the last time I ate?* She didn't want to go out. *I can go another day without food. I don't have much of an appetite, anyway.*

* * *

"So, you make people feel better, Doc?" He had asked her, that first day they met. The session had taken place in her large Philadelphia office. His deep brown eyes had been so wide and desperate, like a trapped animal, seeking cover from attack.

"I try," Abby replied with a cautious smile. "I can only guide you. Whether you get better will depend on how much you are willing to participate in the process."

"I'll do anything," he said, as fresh tears filled his eyes. "Oh please, Doc, I just want my life back. I just want these horrible feelings to go away. I will do anything you say."

And he did. He had followed his therapy goals, confronted his demons, and confessed atrocities committed in the name of war. At only twenty-six, he was a young man. He had been deployed for a little over a year; much less than most of the patients she treated. But this man, Bill Neil, was different. What he had done in the name of his country broke him in a very deep way. He confessed, through deep, gut-wrenching sobs, he had liked the brutality. He returned from war craving it. There was exhilaration in the "release" he felt when he took the life of another.

"It's okay." The words she had spoken echoed through her mind as her own body shuddered with the force of her grief. "It's normal to feel that way," she assured him.

It was that very moment which haunted her. Those whispered words meant to soothe him, meant to steer things back into proper perspective for a young man who had committed no greater crime than following orders. As Abby recalled the memory, tears streamed from between thick lashes framing her eyes. The intensity of that moment washed over her yet again. Remorse threatened to cripple her, to rob her of any remaining sense of self-worth. So, she decided it was time to get up, to get out and avoid obsessing, as she would advise anyone else to do. Abby forced herself out of bed and into the small bathroom cubicle for a brief shower. Once dressed, she trudged back out through the houseboat's front door.

* * *

» Chapter 2 «
~RUMBLINGS~

It was a beautiful Sunday morning; almost midday by the time she emerged into the sunshine. The tiny town her uncle had insisted she visit was moving at a slow pace matching the sun's movement across the sky. There were very few cars on the road. Abby noticed right away that several of the stores on the main strip were closed. She hadn't even considered the idea there might not be anywhere to buy groceries.

Abby's trip had been made in a daze. She had flown into Eugene, Oregon and then taken a pre-booked Budget Taxi to her uncle's boat, assuming she would not need a car. As she stood outside a tiny shop, displaying food in the window but with a closed sign on its door, she wondered if she would have better luck finding a car rental. Her eyes scanned to the end of the strip, where she noticed a diner that appeared to be open. Her stomach growled again in encouragement. *The last thing I need is to deal with people.* But she was hungry and had no other choice if she wanted to eat.

When she entered, the diner appeared to be crowded with townsfolk. She wondered if this was a routine - brunch after Sunday services - or maybe a matter of it being the only gathering place available. Either way, she felt as if the entire population of Winchester Bay was staring at her when she stepped in. Apparently the residents were not opposed to gawking.

Abby lowered her eyes, pushed back a strand of brown hair that escaped the hairband holding a ponytail, and headed for the only empty table she could find.

"Oh, sorry, Ma'am," a young blond waitress chirped quickly, as Abby was about to sit down. "That table is reserved." Abby was not amused. *Could this be some kind of discrimination against out-of- towners?*

"Can I get something to go, then?" The young waitress looked a little confused by the question.

"That's alright! She can join us," a small voice chimed.

Abby turned to see who had spoken up. It was a little girl with brown curls, swept into two slightly-lopsided pigtails. Her eyes sparkled with the untainted friendliness only a child could possess. She smiled and issued the invitation again. It was only then Abby noticed hands on the child's shoulders, and when she looked up to see who owned those hands, her gaze met Craig Port's eyes.

"Craig?" Abby acknowledged quietly, forcing her lips into a smile. The unfamiliar expression felt very awkward, and it showed.

"Abigail," he replied with a quick wink, "this is my daughter, Chloe." He patted the top of the child's head; she could not have been more than seven. "Would you like to join us for lunch?" He offered as he pulled out a chair for his daughter.

"I don't think that's a good idea," Abby said quickly.

"Oh, please," Chloe begged as she patted the seat next to her. "I heard you're from Philadelphia. Is that true? That's so far away!"

Abby could not imagine how anyone knew anything about her. She hoped they would not figure out who she was. She didn't want her peaceful retreat turned into a media circus.

"I am," she nodded lightly, it was more comfortable to focus on Chloe's transparent face, "and it is."

Abby glanced at the empty chair Craig laid his hands on top of, prepared to pull it out for her.

 "Best food in town," he assured with a smile to the waitress, who was patiently waiting to take their order. Abby looked toward the door of the restaurant and considered leaving. She could not see how sharing lunch with strangers would help her, but the little girl was so sweet.

Abby had always loved children, but her career had been her main focus. It was hard to think of having a child when she dealt with so much daily trauma. It seemed to her it would be impossible to protect a child from all the injustice and violence in the world. Yet Chloe appeared to be thriving. The smells wafting in from the kitchen were making her mouth water, and her stomach grumbled its vote again. Placing her hand over her waist in a futile effort to stifle the sound, Abby nodded her head and forced another strained smile.

"Thank you," she said politely, as Craig held the chair out for her. Abby could not remember the last time a man had shown her such courtesy. She had dated off and on, but never seriously. She was so wrapped up in her profession she never could find room in her life for a relationship. More accurately, she never made it a priority.

"Can I call you Abigail?" Chloe asked as soon as Abby sat down.

"Ms. Miles," her father corrected. "Or, is it Mrs. Miles?" he asked.

"Abby," she avoided the implied question with her answer, and his eyes by looking at the menu. "Abby is just fine," she assured Chloe.

Chloe cast an impish grin at her father; he always insisted she addressed adults properly. It was a rare treat for her to be allowed a bent rule.

As Abby perused the options, she could feel Craig peering over his menu at her. Every time his eyes grazed over her, she felt it, like an itch demanding attention. It was unnerving. She became irritated with the persistent sensation, looked up and caught him studying her.

"Yes?" she challenged.

"Are you staying long?" asked Craig.

Abby clenched her teeth and tried to resist telling him it was not really any of his business. Thankfully the waitress arrived with drinks and took their orders. A welcome distraction before the words could slip out. Abby found it harder to censor herself since her nervous breakdown. She was prone to bursting out with whatever she was feeling, rather than considering whether it was appropriate

"I'll have pancakes and eggs," Abby said quickly, "and some toast." She paused for a moment and frowned. "Can you add a side of bacon, too?"

"Of course." The waitress smiled.

"You're hungry," Chloe said bluntly, while her father ordered for both of them.

"There aren't many places to buy food here," Abby explained.

"Oh... The grocery store is about thirty minutes away. Do you need a lift?" Craig offered

Abby locked eyes with him across the table. There was something about the way he was being so kind; it did not feel completely generous. It was almost as if he was making an excuse to spend more time with her.

"I can take a cab," she said, smiling politely.

"Not today, you can't." He chuckled.

"I'll go tomorrow," she replied with forced evenness, before giving her menu back to the waitress. Craig narrowed his eyes, as if he was trying to figure her out. Abby was already uncomfortable, and worn out from his attention. The food hadn't even been served yet.

"Are you in school?" she asked Chloe, hoping to steer the conversation away from herself.

"Yes, second grade," Chloe grinned proudly.

"Is Mom having a little time to herself this morning?" Abby guessed, thinking it sweet Craig would bring his daughter for breakfast by himself. She thought he must do so frequently, considering they had a table reserved for them.

The pause became awkward as Chloe's previously impenetrable smile faded. Craig cleared his throat and took a sip of water. Abby realized she had touched upon an emotional subject. When Chloe stared down at the table instead of speaking, Abby glanced at Craig for help. Craig's eyes were clouded with sorrow, and his voice warbled as he spoke.

"It's just Chloe and I, now," he said cautiously, watching his daughter. "We lost Rachel a year ago." Abby was mortified she had brought up such a sensitive topic. Of course, there was no way for her to have known. But still, she felt as if she had caused them undue pain on an otherwise cheerful excursion.

"I'm sorry," Abby said genuinely, her voice barely above a whisper. She didn't know what else to say. Abby had spent so much time wallowing in self-pity, celebrating her own pain; she seemed to have dulled her ability to sense the pain of others. She had been focused on her own problems far too long, without having to consider anyone else's.

"It's okay," Chloe said bravely, her voice marred by the barest of trembles. "Daddy says she still watches over me. Right, Daddy?"

Craig nodded and managed a smile. "Of course she does, Chloe. Why don't you tell Abby about the spelling bee?" he suggested.

Abby smiled with gratitude at him for changing the subject. She could not imagine suffering such a loss at Chloe's young age. She had dealt with many patients who had experienced death, but it was never easy to see immense grief, and confusion, in the eyes of a child

"Oh, I am *so* going to win," Chloe stated, without skipping a beat. "I know Kimmy Parks is very good, too, but I have been practicing every day!"

"It's true," Craig chuckled. "First thing in the morning I hear, 'Quiz me, quiz me!'"

Abby smiled fondly at Craig. She had a developing sense of respect for him, knowing he was parenting on his own. She recalled how standoffish she had been with him when they first met, and regretted not being a little more civil.

"Hm, how do you spell 'laugh'?" She asked knowing it could be a tricky one.

"Seriously?" Chloe said with a knowing smirk. "L-a-u-g-h!"

"Very good!" Abby smiled, genuinely impressed. Craig wore a proud smile, clearly content to watch her try, and fail, to stump Chloe a dozen more times. When the food arrived it was a bit of a disappointment to end the game.

As they had bantered words and letters, Abby felt her smile spread to the point it strained her face. It had been so long since she'd had that joyful stretch. Her eyes fluttered closed for a moment before she turned her attention to the food.

As they ate, she felt Craig's eyes boring into her.

His determination to pry into her life was unsettling. Abby spoke as little as possible for the rest of their lunch, only offering polite and kind words to Chloe, who was very talkative. Craig had grown fairly silent as well, and Abby was sure he was looking forward to the meal being over.

When the waitress brought the bill, Abby quickly snatched it and offered her credit card. "It's the least I can do, since you shared your table with me." She smiled.

"Please, let me," Craig protested firmly shooting a glare of warning at the waitress, who he appeared to know very well.

Abby stood from her chair. "Just this once," she stated, "let someone do something for you." She smiled again and Craig was surprised at the warmth in her voice.

After signing for the bill, Abby wiggled her fingers in a light wave to Chloe and headed out the door. She did not get far before she heard small feet running after her. "Abby! Abby! Do you want to come to the lake with us?" Chloe pleaded, reaching for Abby's hand as she caught up to her.

"Chloe!" Craig called sternly as he ran out of the restaurant after her.

Abby laughed as he skidded to a stop beside them, his face burning with embarrassment. "It's okay. She's very sweet," she assured Craig. In fact, it was more than okay. Chloe's infectious happiness was making a difference in the way Abby felt. She could almost breathe without resisting.

"It's not okay," Craig said firmly as he glowered at his daughter. "You should not be running off like that."

Chloe frowned and scrunched up her nose. "I wasn't running off. I was running *to* Abby," she pointed out reasonably.

"Chloe," he warned, raising one finger in the air.

"Alright, alright," she sighed. "I'm sorry, Daddy."

He smiled, annoyance forgotten with her use of the endearment, and wrapped an arm around his daughter's shoulders. "We are headed to Lake Marie, if you'd like to join us."

* * *

» Chapter 3 «
~WALK IN THE PARK~

To see if he was just being polite, or genuinely extending an invitation, Abby dared a look up at him. His smile appeared welcoming. Abby felt better than she had in months, so she decided it might be a good idea.

"Sure. For a little while," she agreed. With a smile at Chloe, she added, "Thank you for inviting me."

Chloe skipped off ahead of them as they walked beside each other. Abby found it interesting how easily they fell into step, their footfalls matching one another's.

"I'm sorry if I brought up a delicate subject," Abby mentioned softly. Craig glanced over at her and she felt the intensity of his inspection once more.

"It's alright," he assured. "It was hard to lose Rachel, of course, and very difficult for Chloe. But, well..." he paused as he looked ahead at his daughter skipping along, "I knew I couldn't dwell on the loss or she would never heal."

Abby canted her head slightly to the side as she looked up at him. "And you? Have you been able to heal?"

His jaw tensed slightly. "Well, I keep myself busy." His voice caught with emotion, then he explained, "I'm in real estate and the demand for housing is actually growing in this area."

Abby noticed how he did not exactly answer her question. "And you like to fish?" She recalled how he had looked the day before. Today he was dressed in slacks and a loose knit top, which was in much better shape. In the absence of his cap, his curls still fell perfectly around his head and brow.

"Yes, I actually spend as much time as I can outside. I'm the volunteer park ranger for our little town," he joked. "I keep an eye on the wildlife, including my daughter." He chuckled.

Abby shared his laugh quietly, a real laugh, not an imitation one. "It's very beautiful here," she said as they stepped onto the sandy beach surrounding the lake.

"It is." He let his gaze linger on the creases and curves of her features. He could not figure out why he found her so intriguing. They fell silent for a few moments as Chloe ran along the shoreline, spooking the birds gathered there.

"You know, most people don't visit here," he said quietly. "There are plenty of more tourist-oriented places to vacation." He kicked his shoe lightly into the sand, leaving an indent.

"Is that so?" Abby mused.

"But you chose to come here," he reminded her.

"Is that a problem?" she asked, with a roughness around the edge of her voice. "Is there a 'no visitor' policy in Winchester Bay?"

Craig winced as he realized he may have pushed her a little too hard.

"I was just trying to learn a little bit about you," he said calmly, as he sought out the cinnamon shade of her eyes. "I didn't mean that as rudely as it came out. You are a bit of a puzzle. An intriguing puzzle." The last said with a sincere smile which almost distracted her from the curious twinkle in his eyes.

Abby sighed and ran the palms of her hands across her cheekbones to clear away the emotions that surfaced when she had been reminded she was just visiting. One day she would have to return to her reality, a place where she no longer fit.

"No, it isn't you," she shook her head. "I'm sorry. I'm not myself right now. I really came here for some isolation. I should probably go." She started to turn away from him and was surprised when his hand encircled the crook of her elbow. It was not a forceful gesture. Still, the physical contact was disruptive, since she had hidden herself away as deeply as possible. The unexpected connection to someone rattled her.

"In my experience," he spoke gently, "nothing good ever comes from isolation."

Abby stared hard at his fingers, gently closed around her elbow. Only then did he seem to notice he was holding her. He pulled his hand away swiftly and his cheeks flushed.

"In my experience," Abby countered, with annoyance coloring her tone, "being nosy leads to knowing things you wish you didn't."

Craig arched one brow at her harsh words. "I wasn't being nosy," he replied, his tone even but his eyes possessing a glint of anger. "Forgive me for taking an interest. I won't make that mistake again."

"Great," Abby smiled tensely.

"Great," he replied curtly, utterly baffled by the entire exchange. Everything about Abby confused him. Since his wife died, he hadn't the slightest interest in another woman and did not believe he ever would. It was not because he was bitter; his life was full, with his daughter to care for, and his work to manage. His love of nature kept him balanced. Craig had not missed that type of companionship. More accurately, he did his best not to slow down long enough so that he would miss it.

He watched as Abby turned and walked back across the sand. He could see in the way her shoulders slumped and the way she walked - her steps were weary - she carried something very heavy with her. *But that's no excuse for being rude*, he told himself.

"What did you do?" Chloe whined when she ran up to her father.

"What did *I* do?" He shot back. "I didn't do anything."

"Yes, you did. You did something," Chloe pouted, pointing to Abby, her figure disappearing across the beach.

* * *

Later that day, Craig dropped Chloe off at her friend's house to play and made his way to the sheriff's station. When he walked in, the sheriff waved him straight into his office.

He hung up the phone, pointing to the chair across from him. "Craig, how are you doing today?"

"Good! Good," Craig said with obvious distraction. "I met the woman who's staying on Pat Miles' boat."

"Right. Abigail, I think?" The sheriff nodded as he glanced over some papers. Neither of them knew Pat very well. He was one of a few residents who came and went when it suited him.

"Yes, Abigail," Craig nodded slowly, his eyes narrowing. "She seems a little strange to me," he frowned and rubbed his chin.

"Strange, how?" The sheriff looked up. He trusted Craig's opinion and often relied on him as an honorary deputy of sorts, to keep an eye on what was happening in the town.

"It's odd, Paul," Craig said as he leaned forward in the worn faux-leather chair. "It's like she's hiding something."

Paul frowned and tapped his fingers lightly on the table. Secrets weren't all bad, he decided. "Well, you know city folk always have some kind of drama, Craig. I wouldn't read too much into it."

Craig shifted in his chair and frowned again. "I just can't shake it," he said quietly. "It's like there's something about her –"

"Oh, I see." Paul drew the words out as he sat back in his chair with a loud squeak of the swivel mechanism. He had been the one to find Rachel the day she died. Dense fog, and terrible weather, caused her to lose control of the car. It was a simple accident, but there was nothing simple about a man losing his wife, or a child her mother. Those types of things did not happen too often in Winchester Bay. It had broken the hearts of every resident.

"You see what?" Craig responded, bristling as he met Paul's eyes.

"Well, Craig, it's been over a year and—"

"And what?" Craig dared him to continue, his jaw clenching.

"Maybe you see something in this woman, something you're interested in?" Paul suggested, cautiously.

Craig burst out with a bitter laugh and shook his head. "Wow, Paul, trying to play matchmaker?" he teased, irritation replaced by a trust in Paul's good intentions.

"Hey, I have nothing to do with your interest in Abigail," he pointed out. "You met her all on your own!"

"Abby," Craig corrected, softly.

"Abby, is it?" Paul replied and tried to hide a grin. "Well, all I'm saying is sometimes life changes the way we think, the plans we make. Sometimes it just sneaks up on us."

Craig started to argue with his friend, but in truth he couldn't completely deny it. When Abby had smiled at him, he liked the way her eyes crinkled at the edges, and how it accentuated the fullness of her lips. He never even noticed those things on other women. Maybe it was his slight attraction to her that made him think she was hiding something.

"Well, either way," Craig shrugged, "I'm not interested in a relationship. I have everything I need in my life."

Paul shuffled the papers on his desk and cleared his throat. He had been very good friends with Rachel as well, and if there was one thing he knew for certain, her first concern had always been Chloe. He knew Craig was doing a great job raising his daughter. But it would break Rachel's heart to think of her daughter growing up without a mother.

"And what about Chloe? Does she?" Paul asked quietly, and then braced himself.

Craig was an even tempered man. He always had been. Even when Rachel passed away, his only reaction had been quiet devastation. He did not bemoan the unfairness of his loss. There was no anger. Instead he had grieved, and then turned his attention to his child. But in that moment, as Paul questioned him, the fury in Craig's eyes was more than evident.

"Don't ever ask me that question again," he said, not raising his voice, but still making his point. Craig rose and glowered at his friend. "I will give Chloe everything she could ever need." With that, he turned and walked out of the office, slamming the door shut behind him. The other officers in the station all looked up with surprise, but they did not question Craig. Everyone understood his right to pain.

Paul sighed as he looked at the door. "Some things can't be given," he murmured to himself. He knew he had crossed a line, but it had been necessary. Craig shut himself down in many ways after Rachel died. Urging him to open back up was something only Paul could do.

* * *

» Chapter 4 «
~PASSAGES~

Abby walked back toward the marina. She was glad to be done with talking, and especially answering Craig's questions. *Why is he so nosy?* Her irritation with him started to subside the moment she walked away. *Why was he watching me?* His incessant prying and scrutiny put a damper on an otherwise delightful visit to the lake. Abby noticed she felt at peace being there. She experienced something else, something which had escaped her for months on end, something she thought she'd never experience again – joy. Thoughts of Chloe playing entered her mind, and she smiled.

No one stopped Abby along the way. No one even said "Hello." She was focused on putting one foot in front of the other, and only that. She was surprised when she came across the marina so soon; she wasn't aware she had been moving that quickly. She couldn't recall hearing anyone, or seeing anyone. It was as though time and space had folded and dumped her there. Abby wasn't particularly lost in thought; this time, it was her thoughts that were lost. For the first time in a long time, her mind had not been flooded with regret; it was rather calm. And that was strange. *Could it be this place?* She mused at how silly Chloe looked as she chased birds along the water's edge, and secretly wished she could have chased them, too. *It was nice to laugh and smile again.*

Abby's thoughts turned to Craig. She was suspicious of him, and uneasy with all his attention. *Why all the pressure? The probing? Could it really be just idle curiosity?* Abby's bark had been more of a knee-jerk reaction. She had been hounded for so long that she suspected everyone's intentions. Her new tendency, toward thoughtless retorts, was the whole reason she stayed on the boat and away from people. *What if he really meant nothing by it?* She cringed, and bit her bottom lip. *Uh, if that is true, then he must think I'm a crazy psycho woman – a certifiable bitch.* Abby felt embarrassed as she realized her reactions were probably over the top. *What do I say if I see him again? "I'm sorry?"*

Abby boarded the aging houseboat and headed for the kitchen, deciding to check it, once again, for food. There wasn't any, and she had no clue where to eat dinner. She didn't want to go back to that diner - it would mean dealing with more people. She was all talked out. Realizing Monday would mean more people in the grocery store, more talking and more questions, prompted Abby to venture out again. *It's still light out. Maybe I can catch a cab?* She wound a scarf around her neck, checked her hair in the mirror, and headed out.

* * *

Craig was furious when he walked out of the sheriff station and onto the street. He knew Paul had meant well, but Chloe's well-being was a very sensitive issue for him. Truth was, it did concern him she might have to grow up without a woman's hand. It pierced him, daily. As he started walking down the sidewalk, hoping to cool off, he saw Abby.

She was standing at the entrance of Bay Harbor, with her purse slung over her shoulder, glancing at her watch. She had been waiting for a cab to take her to the grocery store for over an hour. Twice the dispatcher had called to check the address she had given them. *Twice. What idiots! Apparently Winchester Bay is too tiny for them to find.*

When Craig spotted her standing there, he started to turn away. He did not want to deal with his conflicting emotions about her when his temper was already short. Conversely, Abby saw him walking toward her and sighed with relief. She waved her hand and offered a generous smile, knowing their last encounter had not ended well.

"Hi, Abby," he said courteously. He did not want to be rude. "Is everything okay?"

"No, not really," she frowned. "I know I'm probably not your favorite person right now, but I was wondering if the offer for a lift to the grocery store might still be good?"

Craig swept his eyes over her and drew a slow breath as the last of his anger subsided. He didn't think it was the wisest choice to go off alone with her, but he also couldn't turn down someone who was in need.

"Sure." He nodded. "Chloe's staying with one of her friends, so it'll only be us. Is that okay?"

Abby tensed a little, as she had anticipated the child would be a good buffer. "Actually, maybe I can wait for the cab," she said as her phone began to ring.

Craig smirked, folding his arms as she answered.

"What do you mean, you've given up?" she gasped into the phone. After a few harsh words, she hung up. Biting into her bottom lip she glanced nervously over at Craig to discover he had one brow raised and keys dangling from a fingertip.

"No charge, I promise." He smiled, hoping to ease her tension.

Abby managed a smile in return. "Thanks."

* * *

Craig's truck was more of an SUV; an older model, but very well maintained. Its shiny red paint stood out like a beacon amidst the mild hued cars they passed on the road. Abigail was impressed at how clean he kept his car; even the interior was spotless. Her car, on the other hand, was quite a mess, cluttered beyond belief. She often lived out of it, grabbing a snack on the way to work or picking up dinner on the way home. She had no idea how he kept it so clean when he had a child. Bemused, she looked over at Craig to ask him a question and noticed he was gripping the steering wheel so tightly, his knuckles had gone white.

As he began to turn off the main road, onto the two-laned highway, Craig glanced over at her and his expression darkened. Abigail was a little startled and unsettled by his grimace. She became acutely aware she had accepted a ride from a virtual stranger. No matter how cute his kid was, he was still an unknown. She glanced over her shoulder into the back seat, checking for weapons or any sign she might have made a fatal mistake. As she did, Craig's hand reached across the truck, as if he were grabbing for her neck. Abigail shrank back, her eyes widening with fear. As her lips began to part in preparation to scream, his hand moved past her neck to grasp the seatbelt beside her. He tugged it free of its hook and dragged it across her body. Abby was so flustered she did not even protest or help him push it snugly into its clasp with a snap. She was still staring at him in bewildered shock when his hand settled back on the steering wheel, tightening again.

"You could have just reminded me," she ventured. Her voice echoed with confusion and annoyance. Craig glanced over at her, as if he had not even paid attention to what he had done.

"Oh, sorry." He managed a laugh and shook his head. "Force of habit. I still have to buckle Chloe in. She forgets."

Abby's psychologically investigative mind was working overtime as she studied him. His gaze was concentrated through the windshield, his eyes flickering back and forth, constantly sweeping the road and checking his mirrors. His cheeks were flushed and his jaw was clenched. Abby wondered if this was usual for when he was when driving. *Or, is he nervous because I'm here?*

When they rounded a bend which overlooked the ocean, Abby's breath was taken away. *Whoa! How beautiful.* The sunlight sparkled on the surface of the water, glistening like dancing diamonds, corralled to greet the afternoon sky. It reached endlessly off into the distance, where water merged with the turquoise horizon. Abby wasn't easily moved by nature, but this particular location was spectacular. The magic of the view was accented by a small garden of vividly colored flowers which seemed to serve no purpose.

"Amazing," she uttered to herself. "Does the garden belong to someone?" she asked and glanced over at Craig. He held his eyes to the road, but he had slowed down a little. He refused to look toward the garden she mentioned.

"All of us," he said quietly, with a hint of sadness in his tone. "It was something the community did for Chloe and I, to turn a tragic memory into something beautiful."

Abby's heart began to pump harder as she realized what he was inferring without actually saying. His wife died in a car accident. Abby could easily see how it might happen. The bend veered sharply, and from the shine of the guardrail, she could tell it was newly installed. The day was beautifully clear, but

Abby remembered how dense the fog was at dawn and dusk.

At the time of Rachel's death, there probably hadn't been anything there to shield her from the edge of the cliff. Abby felt her throat tighten. *Such a breathtaking view overshadowed by death.* She shook her head. A strange thought entered her mind which she allowed herself to mull over: *I wonder what Rachel was thinking as she went over the cliff?*

Abby disengaged from that thought and turned her attention to Craig. She was at a loss on how to comfort him, so she did what she had done for many of her patients. She reached out and grasped his hand with a gentle, soothing touch. His hand released the steering wheel, relaxing beneath hers. His jaw rippled as it, too, unwound little. His eyes narrowed some, as if he was attempting to control his emotions. He sighed as he looked over at her.

"Chloe loves to look at the flowers. She calls it her mother's garden. It's remarkable how children innately accept the cycle of life, while we adults flounder and rage against it." He grimaced around his words. Abby was startled by how insightful he was, and by the wisdom in what he said. It was not that she assumed him to be stupid, or less than educated, but she did not expect him to share something he had obviously spent a lot of time thinking about so openly with her.

"I think it's wonderful how the whole community came together for you and your daughter," she said. Abby found it more than wonderful; it was downright fascinating.

She came from a busy city, where very few neighbors even knew each other's name. And she was no different than the rest. She could not put a name to a single neighbor on the street where she lived. By now, they all knew her name. If not, they knew where she lived well enough to target her house with eggs, spray paint, doggie-doo bombs, or bags of garbage. She was disgusted by all the detritus strewn over her front yard. Not that she deserved an outpouring of support.

Scenes from her past echoed in her mind as she slumped down in her seat.

"That's how it is, here," he said casually. The further he drove from the garden, the less intense his emotions became. "It's more than a community; it's like a family." Craig glanced over at her, a light grin tugging at the edges of his lips. "Of course, everyone does tend to be a bit nosy."

Abby blushed as she remembered the final accusation she had lobbed at him when they were at Lake Marie. She had been terrified he would dig too deep, discover too much. She still was.

"Well, you know what they say about outsiders?" Abby attempted a laugh. "Once an outsider, always an outsider."

"Not here," he corrected as he slowed the car at a red light. He glanced over at her and only then did Abby realize she was still grasping his hand. She drew it away, her fingertips dancing nervously across his skin. "Here, they say an outsider is only an outsider until they're part of the family."

Abby folded her hands in her lap, looking at them as if they had done something to offend her. "Well, that's a warm notion, but I'll only be here for a little while."

The light changed and Craig began to drive again, nodding. "As you mentioned. You've yet to tell me why you're here in the first place."

"Just a little time away," Abby replied, managing to make her voice sound friendly enough.

He barely paused before inquiring, "Away from where?"

"From where I was." She cast a saucy smile in his direction. He could prod all he wanted, but he was not going to get much out of her. Craig, enjoying a challenge, was not deterred. He switched lanes cautiously, and then glanced over at her with a glint in his dark green eyes.

"Away from whom?" he boldly cast again.

The question threw her off slightly, as she knew there was only one person she had truly wanted to get away from, the only person she could never escape. She thought about lying, about making up a story about a bad break up and a boyfriend who was too persistent. She thought about flat out demanding he stop asking so many questions. But when he turned the car into the grocery store parking lot, his eyes swept briefly over hers with such warmth and openness, she found herself answering honestly, if cryptically.

"Away from the person I once was," she replied in a soft enough tone he could pretend not to have heard if he chose.

* * *

» Chapter 5 «
~DISCOVERED~

Craig turned off the engine and pulled his keys from the ignition, but he made no move to open the door. Instead, he turned in his seat in an attempt to face her. "Is that person so different from who you are now?" He was insanely curious about this woman's evasive nature. He'd never met someone capable of being so withdrawn, and yet still warm and considerate. It was as if she could listen to his whole life story, feel empathy for him, but never give him the chance to do the same for her.

Abby cringed a little at the intensity of his focus upon her. She began to think he had missed his calling. He would have made a good therapist; he was quite intuitive, and persistent. *He would have done just fine in my field.*

"Not yet," she admitted as she put her hand on the door handle and began to open it. "But I hope one day, she will be." She was about to make a dramatic exit from the car, when she encountered the boundary of the seat belt he had put on for her. He reached out and covered the clasp she reached to release. Abby's cheeks burned with embarrassment.

"I promise you, before you leave here, you're going to tell me everything," he said, with enough lightness to his tone he could get away with such an aggressive statement. He released the clasp on the belt and Abby nearly jumped out of the car in an effort to get away. She did not look back at him, not even when he fell into step beside her. Abby adjusted her purse on her shoulder and grabbed a cart as they reached the entrance. It was about one-third the size of stores she was used to. She was fairly certain they would not have a great supply of the organic foods she usually purchased. Abby tried to quell her anxiousness by building a list in her mind.

As she pushed the cart through the sliding doors, she realized Craig was going to follow her around the store. She usually did not have company while she shopped. There was something intimate about him knowing her purchasing habits. First of all, the number one item was a large bottle of wine. What would he think of her? More importantly, why did she care what he thought? To her relief, the grocery store was more populated than the sleepy town had been. She hoped it would be busy enough to distract him from her selections, and from asking any more questions.

"This you have *got* to try," Craig said with pride, as though she would be missing out on life if she did not taste it. There he stood holding up a large bottle of wine. Abby froze, staring at him with surprise. His smiled faded as he lowered the bottle.

"Oh, you don't drink?" He realized he might have ventured into personal territory. "AA?" He probed.

"No, no," she blurted out as she took the bottle of wine from him. She then lifted one shoulder in a mild shrug. "At least, not yet." Abby laughed awkwardly and looked over the label on the bottle of wine he offered.

"It's from a local orchard," he explained and tapped the glass lightly with his fingernail. "It is delicious. You'll never be able to get it back in Philadelphia. So you'd better enjoy it while you're here."

Abby gave him a small smile before setting the bottle of wine into her grocery cart. "Thanks," she said and continued down the aisle. A woman walking toward them met eyes with Craig and flashed a secretive grin. Craig glanced away, pretending to look at the selection of rice.

"Oh boy, we're going to be the talk of the town," he muttered as he shook his head. "That was Penelope Baker, the mayor's wife. Before we get back, everyone will know we were caught in the act," he gasped and clutched at his chest playfully, "of grocery shopping together."

"Oh, if it bothers you, maybe we should split up," Abby suggested, trying to hide the hopefulness in her voice. Craig cast her a sidelong look which was more mischievous than intimidating.

"And miss out on investigating your food preferences? No way." He shook his head firmly, sweeping his fingers back through his brown curls. Abby sighed in surrender and began looking through the choices of salmon.

"I thought you said you were a volunteer park ranger, not a volunteer detective," Abby grumbled, shuffling through fish until she found one that was the right size.

"You know, I could catch one of those for you," he pointed out with a chuckle.

"Oh yes, I forgot. You are a fisherman, too. My, aren't you a jack of all trades!" Her tone mostly teasing, she placed the salmon next to the wine and continued her browsing. As she chose some berries and vegetables, Craig wandered off briefly. When he returned, he had two large containers of chocolate ice cream. Abby looked up at him, puzzled.

"One's for you, and one's for Chloe," he explained. "Do you mind if I leave it in your cart?"

"That's fine," Abby smiled. The more time she spent with Craig, the more she found him endearing. Although his constant questioning was not pleasant, his general nature was kind and warm. Considering his horrific loss, she couldn't imagine a person more grounded. He really did seem to be capable of living his life, of being happy. A slight twinge reminded her she did not just admire his personality. Craig was quite interesting and, despite herself, she was beginning to find him rather attractive. She shook off the thought with a shrug and a chuckle. She had no intention of pursuing him. But it was reassuring to know she could actually feel interest. *Maybe, just maybe, one day I will have something of a life again.* She was not convinced.

* * *

The rest of the grocery trip went by pretty swiftly, as she was sensitive to the fact Craig would have to get back to Chloe. As she stacked her items on the conveyer belt to check out, Abby purposely avoided looking at the magazines and newspapers lining the lane. She disagreed strongly with what they pushed; lies to make a quick buck.

Abby began to notice whispers between the beeping of the food scanner. As she rummaged in her purse for her wallet, she felt her stomach suddenly clench.

"Is that her?" The whisper came from somewhere nearby. Sure, they could have been talking about anyone, but Abby doubted it. She was positive they were discussing her. *How do they know who I am, way out here?* It became harder for her to concentrate on getting her credit card out of her wallet as the whispers continued. Being talked about took you right back to high school. Gawd did she hate that feeling... being chided, feeling self-conscious. She finally wrestled her credit card out of its little slot and handed it impatiently to the woman at the cash register. Her anxiety was growing.

Abby became increasingly uncomfortable, shifting from foot to foot, averting eye contact. Her cheeks were flushed, her eyes watered and her breathing became shallow. She had to get out. *Could the checker ring any slower?* She didn't want to be discovered. A feeling of impending doom built deep in Abby's gut. She dared not look up. She wanted to escape the store, to become invisible, to fade away, but needed the groceries. *Hold on, Abb. Hold on. Breathe.*

Abby's distress mounted, knowing those people, and more importantly, Craig, were standing right behind her. *Does he know they're talking about me? He is so silent.* Abby decided to risk a glance. As she turned to steal a look at Craig, she was stricken by what she saw. Just beyond him, close to the conveyer belt, was a stack of tabloids. And there, splashed across the front page, was her face. The photo couldn't be more unflattering. There she was... stunned, staring helplessly at the cameras as the photographers behind the lenses hounded her. *Damn paparazzi.* The feeling in that moment – the flood of panic and embarrassment – forever immortalized on film, washed over her anew. Abby shuddered. It was a memory she'd like to forget, a memory that haunted her, a memory that cut like a knife. She was both humiliated and traumatized at the thought of it. It was at that moment the whole world had come to know her name.

The headline read, "Where is Abigail Miles? Has She Disappeared?" *What? I'm not some child on a milk carton.* Abby was not being hunted for the sake of wanting her back. The smaller print beneath the ugly photograph made it clear.

"Will the country's most hated psychologist ever show her face again?"

Abby cringed as she saw Craig's hand reach for the paper. *Is he really going to buy that?* Her cover was blown. Everyone in the grocery store now knew who she was and why she was there, including Craig.

"I'm sorry, Ma'am," the clerk said quietly. "Could you swipe the card again? It didn't read the first time." The clerk glanced nervously from Abby to the line of people which had formed behind her. Abby's hand shook as she ran the card again, trying not to look at anyone. She wanted so desperately to get out of the store that she couldn't see straight. Tears were filling her eyes and she was losing it. She was embarrassed, hurt, trapped. Her heart ached and felt as if it was being torn from her chest. She couldn't stand it. *Please, please, please... can this end?*

The receipt finally began to print. Abby snatched it from the clerk and impatiently tried to pack the cart. She glanced back at Craig briefly, watching as he flipped the paper over. He put it back on the stack so her face was hidden. He paused to pay for his ice cream, but Abby could not wait any longer. She had to get out – the stress was suffocating. Abby scurried out of the grocery store, not realizing she had left her bags.

Abby stood outside, her mind flooded with jumble of disconnected thoughts. As she paced back and forth on the sidewalk outside the store, she was in a near panic. *They know who I am? How will I face them? And Craig... will he tell anyone? Will he keep my secret? Heck, will he even give me a ride home, knowing who I am?* She didn't think so, and only then remembered she had left her groceries inside. *Stupid, stupid, stupid. What am I going to do? I can't go back in!*

Abby was so frantic she couldn't think straight. She rounded the corner of the store, thinking only of getting away. *I could certainly call a cab from here... or just walk. I'll do anything to not face Craig again.* She struggled to keep the tears from streaming down her face. Once more, she felt like a specimen under a microscope. She was breaking down, again. *Oh please... I don't want to go back to the sanitarium. Maybe I can run away?* Dark thoughts flooded her with such rapidity she couldn't help but loathe herself. Abby was so swept up in a tsunami of pain and self-doubt she couldn't form a rational thought. It was the hand on her arm that snapped her back into reality

"Abby!" Craig said in a forceful tone. "Breathe... just take a deep breath." He struggled to meet her eyes but held her gaze once he found it. His hands cupped her face.

"Ready? Breathe with me." He took a deep breath in, and blew it out. It was calming. Abby fought it. She didn't want to breathe. She wanted to disappear. She didn't want to be shown kindness. She didn't deserve it. Torrents of tears flowed the moment Craig said her name. His touch was unbelievably comforting. It was the first time, in a long time, anyone had offered her genuine comfort.

"Breathe, I said." Craig was harsher in his tone this time, holding her face firmly. Abby drew in a ragged breath. It felt like spikes lined with razor blades slashing every part of her lungs. She hated panic attacks; they were the scariest thing she had ever experienced. She had never had them, until the event. Abby didn't know what she hated most - the crushing pressure in her chest, the tightening of her throat, the uncontrollable racing of her heart, or the agony of each breath she took. It was like dying a slow, painful, and terrifying death, except death did not come. She was free to be tortured endlessly by the same scenario, each episode no less frightening.

"And again," Craig said, demonstrating how to draw a long, slow breath. His grip loosened on her jaw as she followed his directions. Abby began to feel a little more in control of herself, though it was hard for her to keep calm. Craig walked her through a panic attack. That was even more mortifying than his knowing who she was. Looking down, her embarrassment grew as she saw her bags abandoned on the sidewalk at his feet.

"Shh." Craig moved his thumbs to brush away the tears which had snaked down Abby's cheeks. His subtle touch soothed and scared her in the same moment. It left her in a place of awe. As he tucked wayward strands of hair from her ponytail back behind her ears, he continued studying her eyes, looking for a sign she had fully returned. Abby was grateful for his kindness, but felt exposed. She wanted nothing more than to get as far away from him as possible. His understanding would not last. She feared seeing disgust surface in his expression, as it had in the face of every person who learned the truth of what she had caused.

* * *

» Chapter 6 «

~PARIAH~

"Are you okay?" He was careful not to offend. "I mean, do you think you can get to the truck?" Obviously she was not okay.

Abby nodded quickly. It would be hell to wait for a cab in the parking lot, everyone would stare at her. She was better off getting back to the houseboat, lickety split. She'd have to figure out from there what her next step would be. Craig picked up the bags at their feet and slid an arm loosely around her waist to help her toward the vehicle, shielding her from the onlookers' stares. He stowed the groceries in the back, climbed into the driver's seat and started the engine. He was about to put it into drive when he reached over, grabbed her seat belt, drew it across her and clasped it without ever looking at her. Putting the transmission in gear, he then drove out of the parking lot.

The silence on the way back was deafening, interrupted only by Abby's rattled breathing. She tried to even it out, but the more she attempted to control it, the jerkier it became. Craig cracked a window to let some fresh air into the truck. The noise seemed to drown out her awkward breathing. Abby felt as if she were right back in Philadelphia, reliving it all. She knew, without hesitation, it would not be long before the whole world knew where she was and reporters would again be at her door.

* * *

"It's normal to feel that way," she had murmured, so soothingly. A million times since that morning she had wished she could go back and change those words. If she had told him how atrocious and horrible it was for him to fantasize about such things, maybe that would have been enough to steer him off the path his twisted mind had placed him on. Hindsight was cruel.

* * *

"Abby... I'm sorry," Craig said quietly.

"For what?" she responded in feigned ignorance, her voice shaky.

"For trying to force you to tell me," he glanced her way. "I didn't realize what you were dealing with... I kept asking so many questions. Forgive me."

Abby turned to stare out the window, bracing herself for the inevitable. She tried to hide her concern that he would never want to ask her another question. She knew rejection all too well. But before she could set up her defenses, Craig did ask another question. One he expected an answer to.

"What actually happened?" He tried to give her privacy to answer, keeping his eyes on the road.

"You saw the article," she countered.

Craig shook his head, cocking it slightly to one side. "Right. You coaxed a damaged man into committing mass murder. Am I supposed to believe aliens had Elvis' baby, too?"

Abby felt uneasy he could make a joke so easily about such a tragic event. "It doesn't matter." She shrugged listlessly.

They were nearing Winchester Bay. Abby was aching to get out of the truck, away from Craig and his questions. But most assuredly, away from his assessing eyes.

"Abby, you don't really believe any of that do you?" His tone changed. He slowed the vehicle down, almost to a stop, as he looked over at her.

"All of America does." Her laugh was brittle as she held her hands up slightly, as if to say she couldn't disagree.

"Abby, it's not your fault. You know that, don't you?" Craig tried to meet her eyes but Abby refused to look directly at him.

"If not mine, then whose?" she tested.

Craig was stunned by her reaction. In the article he had read, very briefly, it detailed how Abby experienced a nervous breakdown after the explosion. Since being released from a mental hospital, she had disappeared without a trace. He had assumed it was to hide out from the press, but now, as he watched another tear meander down her cheek, he realized it was because she believed everything they said. When he pulled into a parking space beside the marina, she practically fell out of the passenger door in her haste. He opened the back, ready to carry her groceries in for her, but she refused.

"Please," she said, too ashamed to look at him, "I need some time by myself." She cleared her throat and then added quickly, "Thank you for driving me." After taking the groceries from his hands, Abby hurried off to her uncle's boat. She could feel Craig's gaze trailing after her; its subtle caress clung to her back.

As soon as the door closed behind her, Abby abandoned her groceries and began pacing the length of the little floating house. The urge to get on a plane and fly as far as she could was strong. But, there would be no place she could go. The truth was her patient committed a heinous crime. The world needed someone to blame, and she happened to be it. Abby joined them, blaming herself as well, which made evading the situation even harder.

She picked up her phone, prepared to book a ticket on the next flight out of town, when she noticed the bottle of wine Craig had selected for her, peeking out of the top of her grocery bag. The memory of his kindness calmed her raging emotions, and she put the phone down. *Maybe I just need to relax tonight and see how I feel in the morning?* The sun was setting and the marina was quiet, but for the lapping of the water against the boat. It was her time, her space, her refuge... for now. There weren't a dozen media vans surrounding her, as there would potentially be if she went to the airport.

* * *

Abby saw Bill a few weeks ahead of schedule, as per his request. She had no idea what she was walking into. He was particularly distraught and tense. His brow was furrowed over squinted eyes as he restlessly paced around her office.

"They're calling me a hero. They want to give me a medal. And for what? Senseless slaughter?" His tone was angry. "Will this nightmare ever be over?"

Abby tried to calm him; assure him that this too would pass. It was a patronizing part of the political process... renewing society's hope the cause was honorable. But as it turned out, that really wasn't what had upset Bill the most.

"They came to offer me a job today, but I turned them down," Bill revealed.

Abby knew he had been between jobs and really wanted something steady soon. It concerned her he declined an opportunity.

"What? A job? Who offered you a job?" she probed for more details. "And you turned it down?"

Bill tried to regain some composure. He leaned against her mahogany librarian desk, looking down. He took a deep breath in and slowly released it, blowing air out through pursed lips. His head dropped with a negative shake. A few seconds passed before he took in another deep breath, then looked up at Abby and spoke.

"I don't know who they really were – they use fake names, fake credentials - but they said they represented a recruiting arm of Blackwater."

"Black who?" Abby asked.

Bill didn't know if he should say more, but continued anyway. "They said they were pretty impressed by what I'd done in Iraq, and wanted me to work for them." He paused, tears welling up in his eyes. "Impressed? Impressed were they?" His tone grew louder. "I'm a soldier. I'm no fucking merc. I don't kill for hire." Bill was becoming angry, belligerent.

"Who do they think they are?" Tears rolled their way down his cheeks. "I'm no monster," he professed through sobs. He had often talked about seeing the faces of his fallen comrades. Their bodies with holes blown in them, blood gushing out, and body parts missing. It disturbed him. All that death and killing didn't make any sense. War didn't make any sense.

Abby focused on containing the session, holding a calm space. Her job was to anchor Bill and give him a safe place to release. She felt a kernel of satisfaction once his anger seemed contained, and the anguish subsided.

"I grew up caring for people, for my country. How dare they!" Bill felt it was the ultimate insult.

"Is this how they see me?" Bill looked at Abby, tilting his head and furrowing his brow. Abby remained silent and allowed him to vent. His expression then turned quizzical. "Wha... what if they know something I don't know about me?"

"Could they have done something to me, turned me into something that is... not me?" Bill shuddered to think that were possible. He had heard of mind control experiments and thought it was all hocus pocus, sci-fi crap. But now he wasn't sure. *Could we all have been government sponsored lab rats?* Bill became uneasy as paranoia took root in the pit of his stomach. His mind raced, recalling the hundreds of hours of "programming" and myriad of vaccines he had received. *Only God knows what shit was in them. But could that possibly be true? Could it?* A feeling of dread swept over him yet he decided not to verbalize his fear. As he looked at Abby, her expression was indulgent, but patiently detached. She clearly hadn't a clue about what he was saying.

The session wound down. Abby set another appointment for Bill in a few weeks' time. He felt it was sufficient. He knew she had another client waiting, another soldier. As he was leaving, obviously disgruntled and perturbed, but in a better space, he thanked her for her time. As she went to pick up the ringing phone, he looked around her office, as though seeing it for the last time. Under his breath, Bill quietly muttered, "If they want to see a monster, I'll show them one."

* * *

Chapter 7

~SHADOWS IN THE DARK~

Winchester Bay had been a good reprieve. Abby cherished her time there. She feared gossip would spread like wildfire and cause her haven to turn to hell. But, maybe she could squeeze one more night of anonymity out of the town. She turned on some soft music and poured herself a large glass of wine. Incentive to coax her into putting the groceries away. While tucking the ice cream in the very small freezer, she noticed she had two half-gallons. Craig had somehow put his in with hers. Actually, she thought with a warm memory of haphazard pigtails, it was Chloe's ice cream. *Drat! I'd hate for her to miss out on a special treat because of me.* Abby sighed. She really didn't want to go out. But, she wanted Chloe to enjoy the ice cream her daddy had picked. She could easily walk it over to Craig's place. The town was small, and on the walk to the lake Chloe had pointed out which street their home was on. She had been so adorable reciting her house number and street name, more evidence of Craig's thoughtful parenting. *Wouldn't that be the right thing to do, after all he has done for me?*

* * *

Paul stood on the porch with Craig, running his fingers through graying hair. "And you're sure it's her?"

"Yes, of course." Craig's tone was emphatic; frustrated he shoved his hands deep into his pockets. "I saw her face. Her name's on the front of the paper."

"Well, I'll be," Paul shook his head slightly. "I never made the connection. Some law man I am." He chuckled.

"There's nothing funny about this," Craig insisted. "We have to do something to protect her."

"Protect her from what?" Paul asserted as he glanced down the deserted street. "It's not like folks around here are going to string her up or anything. These people understand the poor woman's been through enough."

"Maybe not," Craig said, "but someone might decide to tell the press where she is. Then reporters will flood this place like piranhas.

Abby paused beside the porch. She had walked up to the house from the side of the street. Confirming her memory of Chloe's recitation, Craig's last name, Port, was proudly displayed on the mailbox. However, when she heard voices, she paused, wondering if she should turn back.

"Well, there's not much we can do about that," Paul replied, adjusting the gun on his hip. Abby could see his uniform in the porch light. *Has Craig called the police about me?* Suddenly she wished she had never left the boat. The ice cream was melting fast and her heart was racing.

"There must be something we can do? We can't just let this happen!" Craig said with concern in his voice. "This is our town, and we protect our own, don't we?" he asserted.

Abby misinterpreted his words to mean he wanted to protect the town from her presence. Her mind spun. *How stupid of me.* She thought of how she had been taken in by Craig's kindness. But it was all an act.

"Craig, calm down," Paul warned. "You don't want to get Chloe upset. She doesn't need to know about any of this. I'll see what I can do at my end. But really, there isn't much I can do until something happens."

Abby started to turn away, not wanting to be caught listening in. She didn't want to pollute their town with her presence. As she walked away, she stepped on a dry twig. Its cracking signaled her presence and caught the attention of both men.

"Who's there?" Paul called out sharply, his hand resting on the butt of his gun. Abby winced. She knew if she bolted off now, she would run the risk of being shot. At the very least, she'd get tackled.

"It's me," she said quietly, before reluctantly stepping into the soft glow of the porch light. She held out the barely frozen ice cream in front of her. "You forgot this," she said in explanation. Craig rushed down from the porch and relieved her of the squishy box.

"Abby, I'm glad you're here," he said quickly.

"Don't," she protested and shook her head. "You don't have to pretend to be nice. I'm going to leave in the morning. So, really, there's no need for you two to worry about the town."

"What?" Craig's confusion surprised her. He knew who she was.

"Here. Let me take that inside," Paul offered knowingly. He carried the dripping ice cream into the house, leaving the two of them alone in the front yard. Abby started to turn away once he was gone, but Craig moved swiftly, blocking her departure with his body.

"Why would you leave?" he asked, looking hurt.

"Obviously I'm not wanted here," Abby was desperately trying to hold back tears of disappointment.

"What makes you think that?" Craig demanded, raising his voice slightly.

"You two talking -"

"About protecting you!" Craig emphatically clarified with both hands in the air. "Abby, I was asking if there was a way he could shield you from media attention, that's all. You must have heard us wrong." He reached for her hands when she started to cross her arms, pulling her closer to him. "Abby, you can do what you want, whatever you feel comfortable with. But this town will take care of you. I will-"

"Daddy?" Chloe rushed down the steps of the front porch, already in her pajamas. Her hair was wet from a bath. "Is that Abby?" She squinted through the darkness. "Are you going to have ice cream with us?" she asked excitedly.

"Is she?" Craig asked, just as eager, turning to look back at Abby. She smiled tentatively, having been through too many different emotions for one day. The truth was, ice cream sounded really good to her. Compared to Craig's warmth, and Chloe's enthusiasm, the houseboat seemed very lonely.

"Maybe a quick bite." Abby finally nodded, making Chloe squeal with happiness. She charged back into the house, nearly knocking Paul over as she rushed past him. Paul laughed and tried to pat her head, but she was too fast. He descended the steps of the porch and paused beside Abby and Craig.

"Listen," he said quietly to Abby, "I know you're in the middle of some kind of mess. But as long as you're in this town, it's our job to protect you. So, if anyone gives you any trouble, you let me know, alright?" He met her eyes boldly.

Abby had never met this man before tonight, and yet here he was, offering to protect her, like she mattered to him. She did not know exactly what to say. All she could come up with was, "Thank you, sir," in a stumbling voice.

"Okay, very good. You remember... any trouble, you call me." He slipped her his card and gave her shoulder a light pat before heading down the road.

"See?" Craig pointed out, hoping she would get the message she was welcome

"Craig, when people find out... " she shook her head. "No one can forgive such a thing."

Craig parted his lips as if he had a lot more to say, but then he seemed to change his mind. "Abby, let's go eat some ice cream." He offered her his arm. It hovered in the air for a few seconds before Abby hesitantly took it. After what had happened in the grocery store, she had never expected her night to end like this. But, being here was a lot better than a lonesome bottle of wine.

* * *

For a few minutes, while they chatted together over ice cream, Abby was able to forget who she was. That time meant the world to her. By the time Chloe fell asleep on the couch, she and Craig had polished off the remainder of the ice cream. She felt a little embarrassed when she realized it.

"I'll have to buy you some more," she said apologetically.

"Sure," Craig grinned as he leaned against the counter, "only if you promise to share it with us."

Abby's smile reached her eyes this time, adding a lovely twinkle to their warmth. "Maybe," she playfully hedged.

"Do you want to crash here tonight?" Craig offered, knowing she had walked. Even though the town was safe, he would never leave Chloe alone to escort her back to the marina.

"No," she shook her head. "No, I do my crashing alone," she joked, but it was an honest answer. She also had a bottle of wine waiting for her. "I'll be fine," she promised him.

As she walked home in the crisp night air, she noticed the stars above her. They carpeted the sky and shimmered perfectly, as if positioned just for her. She could not help but think of all the times she had lost herself in the night sky, imagining romance as young women do. Once, she had allowed herself to dream that one special person out there existed for her. All the movies told her so. All the storybooks did, too. She had been convinced her one perfect mate would show up and sweep her off her feet. But, at some point, she had come to realize it only happened in movies and books. The more she learned about psychology, the more misleading she found those movies and books to be. Still, some part of her subtly ached for that dream to come true. She wanted to have hope again.

Distracted with her thoughts, she did not see the flashlight beam bouncing as someone ran away from the marina. She didn't notice the paper tacked to her door until she was turning the handle. It was the tabloid from the grocery store. Scrawled across her picture, in bright red lettering, was a message for Abby.

"No killers in this town!" it read. The note seemed to have been written in lipstick. Abby's hand shook as she pulled the paper down. Intellectually, she knew she should not let it get to her, it was to be expected. But, she could not stop the tears from flowing. She dropped the paper on the deck, rushed inside the cabin and locked the door behind her.

* * *

The problem with staying on a houseboat is it isn't easy to pretend you're not home. Abby didn't have many places to hide. Any movement she made could easily be heard from outside the door. Craig glanced down and saw the newspaper. He picked it up and read the hateful note. That someone in his town would do such a thing annoyed him. But kids were kids and old biddies were old biddies everywhere. There wasn't much he could do.

"Abby." He knocked hard on the cabin door. "Abby, I'm not going to let you hole yourself up in there. You need to come out. Let's talk about it."

Abby rested her forehead against the door, letting his voice wash over her. Unlike before, his words did not soothe her; they enraged her. She had created a nice safe space. She had built a wall protecting herself from the outside world. But dammit if he wasn't determined to push his way through. The bottle of wine she had polished off the night before had done nothing but make her feel slightly woozy this morning.

"I don't want to talk anymore," she said back through the door. "Leave me alone."

Craig set his own forehead against the outside of the door, hearing how close she was to it. "I can't do that, Abby. I need to know you're okay."

Abby abruptly pulled the door open, causing him to stumble and nearly fall into her. "Are you suggesting I might hurt myself?" she asked, glaring at him.

"I just… " he swept his gaze over her pale face and rumpled hair, "I wanted to make sure you were feeling okay."

Abby laughed as she sank down into a small chair beside the door and swept her hair up from her shoulders. With her hair in her hands, she used her right hand to slide the black scrunchie from her left wrist over, quickly tying up her hair.

Feeling tipsy, she wagged her finger to accentuate each of her words. "The key is not to feel, Craig. Haven't you figured that out yet?"

Craig frowned in a paternal manner as he noticed the empty bottle of wine on the small kitchen's counter.

"I was hoping to share it with you," he gently critiqued.

"Right. Because in your pretty town, with your pretty smile, everything is made better with good intentions, isn't it?" She smirked and shook her head. "Craig, this doesn't get swept under the rug. What happened won't ever change."

Craig narrowed his eyes. "I know all about things never changing, Abby. But I also know about not letting the things I cannot control ruin my life. I chose to move forward, not look back."

Abby wanted to be angry with him. She wanted to order him off the boat. But she couldn't. There was something about him that soothed her, in a way no one ever had. His presence, though irritating at times, offered her solace. The way he, and Chloe, made her feel was the peace she sought when she came to Winchester Bay.

"It's a little more complicated for me," she said defensively.

"Really?" he shot back. "Because I don't think there's much more complicated than a little girl growing up without a mother."

Abby swallowed hard and then stood so she could be face-to-face. "Chloe has lost a lot, Craig, but she has you. The people my patient killed? Most of them also had families. I'm not the one who caused your wife's death, but I am the one who caused the death of several parents, and even two children. So please, don't tell me it can be simple, that I can walk away from all of it and live my life. People are right to remind me of who I am! People are right to judge me." She blinked back tears, determined to keep control of her emotions.

"No, Abby," he countered, reaching for her hand, "they're trying to make sense out of something horrible. Wanting to find an explanation that makes it less random. I know. I've done it, too. But it doesn't work. In the end, nothing changes what has happened, or who is to blame."

Abby's eyes widened slightly as she studied him. His words triggered the therapist in her. *Was it possible he blamed himself for Rachel's death?*

"Please, come with me," he invited. "Chloe's at school and I have the day off. I want to show you something, a place that's special to me. I think you might like it, too."

The last thing Abby wanted to do was go out and face the world. But the psychologist Craig had awakened with his words, nagged her. Usually, the last thing you want when you are depressed and anxious, is exactly what you should be doing.

"Fine," she agreed, but didn't seem overly pleased. Craig, thrilled to have her consent, didn't mind her hostility as he led her off the boat.

* * *

» Chapter 8 «
~WHERE GODS PLAY~

According to the compass on his rear view mirror, Craig drove north, then a bit west, pulling into a small off-road parking lot that seemed out of place. As he exited the truck, Abby noted her surroundings. There were no amenities, no benches, not even a garbage can. *What have I gotten myself into?* Craig motioned her toward a small brown sign, a trail marker. She followed him onto the path, her eyes glued to the trail, avoiding obstacles; she followed his footsteps for several minutes. Abby stopped abruptly to survey their destination and was completely taken aback. The trailhead led to a large expanse of sand, reminiscent of desert; sand that seemed to go on forever. The hills and gullies appeared to undulate, as though they were a creature responding to the whims of the wind and the sea. As if the waves had breached the sand, and with the help of the wind, molded the land; then continued to roll. Abby had never seen anything like it, never felt anything like it. It was quiet here, peaceful and serene, empty yet full. It called to her...

The terrain was barren, sparsely populated with tufts of grasses and conifers. Small pools of water – undoubtedly trapped by the sand – formed private little swimming holes. The air smelled crisp, clean and salty; the distant sound of the ocean rushing, an inviting serenade. A gentle breeze whistled a song to be felt, not heard. The sun warmed the scene just so, complimenting perfection. Not a soul was in sight. Seagulls cackled overhead, her only companions aside from tracks left by a cottontail long since gone, and Craig. Abby sighed as she took in a deep breath of the cool, fresh ocean air. She was lost in the moment and embraced it. A kindred spirit lived in this place. It pulled her close to its bosom, and she wanted to stay.

Craig reached for her hand. He tried to hide his surprise when she allowed him to take it. Loosely clasp, together they walked to the peak of one of the larger dunes, one with a perfect view of the beach.

"This is where I come, sometimes," Craig admitted, "when I need a reminder."

"A reminder?" Abby asked. She watched the way the ocean stretched out, unending. The varied blues of the sky reminding her how vast their world was. It was exhilarating to not feel trapped, or held down.

"Even though the grief, the pain, the injustice of it all seems endless, in perspective it's just one grain of sand," he spoke gently. Then he crouched down, still holding her hand in his. With his other hand, he swept up a handful of sand and held it out to her. She crouched down, joining him.

"To us, the hurdles in our lives are as fierce and as huge as the ocean. But to the ocean, our problems are as tiny as one grain of sand." He glanced up at her to see if she understood, or even agreed. Abby watched the sand trail through his long fingers. It was soothing to watch all the little specks disperse so easily, and think of them as her challenges. But her burdens were not made from sand, nor were they mere waves. They would not disappear so easily.

"What if your problem is a tidal wave?" Abby questioned in a whisper, pulling her eyes from the falling sand to meet his tender gaze. "Wouldn't you be better off letting yourself drown than fighting the inevitable?"

"Never!" he replied, as he stared passionately back at her. "Never, because it takes every single one of these grains of sand to create this paradise, Abby. And you're part of it. No matter how much you think differently... you are part of someone's paradise."

Abby laughed at that idea and shook her head as a light breeze blew the ends of her ponytail across her face. "No, there's no one like that in my life."

"Not even your family?" Craig asked carefully. "Not even one little girl, who looks at you and thinks you are the most amazing woman she has ever met?" Abby cringed; she knew he meant Chloe. Then he inched a little closer, his lips dangerously near hers. "Or a man who never thought he could care so deeply about anyone again?"

Before she could answer, his lips caressed hers gingerly in the most tentative of kisses. There was barely any pressure to it, more of a light touch, like the trail of a fingertip. Abby had dated a few men, but never in her life had she been kissed so subtly, so sweetly.

"Craig," she whispered as he drew his mouth away from hers, "I'm not who you think I am," she insisted, her eyes tearing as her gaze met his.

"You are exactly who I *know* you to be," he replied, standing up and drawing her up with him. Before them was the wide expanse of ocean; below them was the rise of sand created by the wind's sheer force. He felt that power surge through him, as if nature had created this place, this moment, just for them. He turned his head to face her once more, as if he might kiss her again, but Abby turned and embraced him instead. She rested her cheek against his, as his arms tightened around her, savoring the connection.

"Craig, I'll never be Rachel," she whispered beside his ear. His entire body stiffened at her words. She realized then she might have said too much. He pulled back from her, abruptly severing their physical connection, and stared hard at the sky above them. She watched a maze of expressions move over his face as Craig weighed his next words.

"Why would you say something like that?" he questioned finally, his voice strong enough to carry over the wind around them.

"Because," Abby winced. She knew what she had to say was not going to make him happy, but felt it needed to be out in the open. He had done so much to help her, perhaps in this small explanation she could give back to him.

"It seems to me like you have it in your head if you find a way to save me, in a way, you'll be saving her."

His face paled. The laughter escaping his lips was more cruel than amused. He shook his head as he glanced away from her. "Wow, you really think you're some great shrink, don't you?" he lifted his gaze, his dark green spheres hardening as they struck hers.

"Craig, I didn't mean anything by it, I just-" Abby floundered as she attempted to explain

"You just thought you had me all figured out," he said quietly, and lowered his eyes back to the ground. A soft breeze swept over the dunes, ruffling his curls. He looked as if he were trying to decide whether to stay, or leave. What he wanted to say, he thought might be better left unspoken. In the end, his need to connect with Abby won out.

"Rachel was an amazing woman." His voice was as a whisper. "She was everything - fun, lively, compassionate, loving." His eyes misted over as he glanced up at Abby, and then away again just as swiftly.

"She was so much more than I could have ever dreamed of. On top of that, she was a wonderful mother." His voice trembled as he took a step back toward Abby. "And do you want to know when I figured all of that out?"

Abby did her best to maintain eye contact despite the raw emotion and fury flooding his gaze. "I figured it all out after her casket was in the ground. Because when she was alive, I was too damn busy to even notice! I was too focused on everything I needed to control, to mold into what I wanted, to even appreciate the amazing woman I had the dumb luck of marrying. So don't tell me I think helping you heal will somehow allay the truth of my own stupidity." Craig deflated before her eyes as he had spoken. Baring himself, cutting open his own heart to show Abby the truth of his loss.

Spent, he continued in a softer voice, "She lived and she died. My biggest regret is I let those precious moments pass me by, as if they were nothing... as if a kiss from her could be routine, as if her love and loyalty was something I expected, instead of savored. So, yes, when I look at you," he swallowed thickly as he swept his gaze over Abby, still confused by the emotions she stirred up within him, "I am thinking of Rachel, but only because I know not to make the same mistake twice."

Abby's eyes flooded with tears as he reached up to cup her cheek with his palm. "But that's it, Craig, I'm none of those things. I appreciate the generosity of your affection, of your attention... But, no matter what you tell yourself, it's never going to change who I am or what I've done."

Craig smiled sadly into her eyes and studied her intently. "One of these days, and hopefully soon, you're going to realize there's nothing about you that needs to be changed, Abby. Because when I look at you, I see truth. When you look at yourself, all you see are the lies they've fed you."

Abby was silent as she stared into his eyes. His words were deep, sweet and loving; she wanted to believe them. She wanted to return to a place where she believed in herself, where she thought she deserved love and would eventually have it. Yet, her life's plan, and every girlish dream, had come to a screeching halt.

"What I did -" she gasped, her body shaking with each word she spoke.

"What he did," Craig corrected her sternly while sliding his hand along the small of her back, swaying her body closer to his, so she could not look away. "What *he* did," he repeated and stroked his gaze across her features, which were crumpled in grief. "You can't take his guilt for him, Abby, no matter how much you want to. 'He was just a kid' - that's what you tell yourself, but you know he wasn't. He was a grown man. He made a terrible choice, not because of anything you did, or said, or didn't say, but because of what he had been forced to do."

Abby shook her head and leaned against the rise of his chest, feeling the warmth of his body seep into her skin.

"I should've been able to help him." She groaned into his shirt. Her body trembled violently at the force of her despair, helplessness tearing through her. "It was my responsibility to help him."

"And you did." Craig inhaled as his arms wound around her, holding her close. "You gave him understanding and a supportive ear. You gave him a place he could feel safe, and shared his pain. You treated him and maintained your professional boundaries. You couldn't do everything for him, Abby – that would be against your profession's rules. You gave all of that to him, but he was the one who refused to embrace it."

Craig paused for a moment. "Why did he refuse it, Abby? Tell me. Why did he refuse your help, your direction on how to reassemble his life?" His tone became a little harsher, indicating he expected an answer.

Abby could only shake her head as she sobbed.

"Tell me, why?" He encouraged, stroking one hand down through her hair, pulling free the tie which held her ponytail so her brown locks could flow down over her shoulders.

Abby's chest heaved with the force of her grief. He grasped her arms gently and pushed her away from his chest, forcing her to look up at him. He did not ask again, instead only stared down into her tear-flooded eyes.

Abby didn't want to face her demons; she'd been running from them for months. It was simpler not to acknowledge the feelings or realizations that burned in her. Craig's words focused what were abstract and distant thoughts. She couldn't contain it anymore; her conscious convicted her. "Because he didn't feel he deserved it. He believed he didn't deserve salvation because he couldn't forgive himself for the things he had done." She reached up to cover her mouth as the dawning horror rushed through her. She was doing the exact same thing.

Craig held her firmly as he looked into her eyes. "And is this how you intend to live the rest of your life?" He watched the eureka moment light up her eyes. "Can you really tell me you believe it is healthy for you to think of yourself that way?" Abby shook her head slightly as her emotions roiled within her, threatening to overflow once more. Craig wound a strand of her hair gently around one of his fingers and gave it a slight tug.

"Punishing yourself will not bring anyone back," he whispered. "Trust me, I have tried." Fresh tears glazed his eyes as he looked at her. "The past is over and done with, Abby. What you have is now, this moment, today, and what it can lead to. Is that something you want to throw away?"

Abby lowered her eyes. She knew his words rang with truth, but was not sure if she could accept them. She had spent so much time believing she was the terrible person everyone had accused her of being. Yet, even now, Craig knew what had happened and he did not see her that way. Since he was one of the kindest people she had ever met, she respected his opinion.

"I think we should go back," she said quietly as she hunched her shoulders against a chilly breeze.

"Abby, I want you to promise me you'll think about all I've said," he requested, as he ran his hands up and down her arms. It wasn't just the chilly air he was trying to warm her from. He wanted to melt the ice she had allowed to build within her heart. Craig knew it was her way of shielding herself from ever feeling again, from being hurt. He thought her choosing to accept responsibility for one man's action was ridiculous. But, he accepted it was a crucial moment of her life. Defined by something beyond her control, Abigail's role as caregiver, as counselor, as confidant, as healer, had taken a dangerous and destructive turn.

"I promise," she agreed, savoring the sensation of his warmth blending into hers. She knew if he held her close a moment longer, she might be the one to take a kiss from him, and perhaps much more. *But would that be right?* She could not believe the impact his touch was having on her.

Craig sighed as he reluctantly pulled away from her. Holding her hand tightly in his own, he led her back to the parking lot. Once she was settled in, he started the truck and tried not to think about how much he hated the idea of driving her home. The ride back was silent but comfortable, both reflecting on the day's revelations. When he parked at the marina, Craig still was not ready to let her go.

"Can I walk you down?" he asked, without looking directly at her. Abby smiled to herself at how polite he was.

"I'd like that," she replied quietly. A moment later he was opening her door. He led her along the dock, and she smiled at the way he kept glancing at her nervously. When they reached the houseboat, he hoped she would invite him in.

"Are you sure you're okay on your own?" he attempted to hint.

"I'll be fine," she assured him and he held her hand as she stepped on to the boat deck.

"Abby, wait," he called out as she walked toward the cabin door. She turned back to face him, her heart racing.

"What is it?" she said hopefully. She could not bring herself to invite him on to the boat, not after how dangerously needy she had felt on the dunes.

"Just, I'm here if you want to talk." His words sounded lame to his own ears.

"Thank you." Abby forced a smile to her lips. She wanted to plead with him to stay, but everything in her mind told her it was a bad idea.

"Alright then," he nodded. "I'll see you soon."

He turned and strode back down the dock. Abby watched him until he reached the parking lot. A part of her wished he would come racing back and demand to be let onto the boat. But Craig was far too polite to do anything like that. And besides, it was probably close to the time for him to pick Chloe up from school. She sighed as she opened the door to the cabin and slipped inside, closing it firmly behind her, and then got ready for bed. It was early to sleep, but her day trip with Craig had been emotionally draining. There was no where she needed to go, and no place she'd rather be, than in a cocoon of pillows and blankets. Maybe she'd emerge as someone different.

Mulling over the day, Abby recalled Craig's touch grazing her skin. How electrified she felt when his lips touched hers. *Is Craig just a distraction? To avoid facing what I left behind?* The thoughts swirling through her mind frightened her. Having been emotionally detached for so long, she wasn't sure she could trust what she was feeling. Abby told herself she hadn't come to this sleepy little town to get involved with anyone, and she had no intention of leaving broken hearts in her wake. She did not want to hurt Craig, or Chloe. There was no way she would risk the hearts of two precious people, even if it meant ignoring the desires of her own. As she fell asleep, she vowed she would no longer allow her emotions make decisions for her.

* * *

» Chapter 9 «
~IN DREAMS~

Abby looked at her phone as it rang again. She knew whose number she would read on the screen. Craig had been calling her twice a day, for the past few days. *He must have gotten my number from the harbor master or Paul.* Without having spoken to him, she knew he was trying to check on her. It was understandable, after sharing such a passionate kiss on the dunes, then barely saying a word on the ride back.

When they had kissed, the intensity of the desire she felt frightened her. She craved him, his touch, the sound of his voice, the solace she obtained when she was near him. She did not trust herself or her feelings. It was all too much, too fast, in her mind. *I'm far too much of a mess to get involved with him.* That was one thing Abby was sure of.

Craig hung up the phone with a sharp jab of his finger. He had called so many times, Abby's phone number was the only one showing up on the list of recent outgoing calls. He was more than frustrated - they had shared such an intimate moment, and now she would not answer the phone.

"I guess that's how they do things, in Philadelphia," he said under his breath as he tossed the phone onto the kitchen table. He grabbed his jacket and stormed out into the backyard to chop firewood that didn't need to be chopped. After Rachel died, he chopped firewood for the whole town, enough to last two winters. When Chloe saw him storm out the back door, she knew what he was going to do, and it left her disappointed. For the first time in a long time, she had seen her father's eyes glowing with happiness. She was sure it was because of Abby.

Chloe smiled a little as she realized how much he must like Abby. She liked Abby too. As she sat down at the kitchen table, she began to devise a simple plan and thought of Paul. *Surely Paul would know what could be done, what would work?* She looked out the window and saw Paul's car coming slowly up the street; he patrolled it about this time every day. Chloe jumped up from the table, grabbed a sheet of her favorite pink paper, then set out to fetch Paul.

By the time Craig came back inside, the house was empty but he could hear Chloe chatting with Paul on the porch. He sighed as he looked around the house. *It sure could use a woman's touch.* He missed having the company of his wife, but for the very first time since her death, he missed the company of another woman. He missed Abby.

* * *

Abby slept a fitful sleep. Unwisely, she'd refused the shrink's medications, and night after night, the dreams came. Others would call them nightmares. The intervals with her eyes closed couldn't exactly be called sleep; it was more like she succumbed to wave after wave of explosive emotion. Exhausted, she was powerless to resist a parade of bad memories. Her mind drifted into a vague semi-conscious sleep state, a world between reality and another dimension. This setting replayed often. Abby was back in her Philadelphia office. She was sitting across from an empty chair, speaking to it, as if someone were occupying the seat.

"Don't do it, Bill. It's wrong," she said sternly. "You're not a murderer; you're a soldier. What you were obligated to do should not change the essence of who you are, deep inside. Remember your desire to protect and serve. It is honorable... "

"Honorable?" Bill said, his voice echoing from the walls behind her. "What's so honorable about killing? People think I'm a hero. Not true. I'm a butcher. " As Abby spun around to face the specter, she struggled to redirect his words, to reframe his experience through what her other patients had shared. The only words she could utter came out unintelligible; she was babbling. Then Bill stated, "I'll show them what I really am, what they made me into."

Suddenly her words were drowned out by the sound of sirens. The perspective and setting changed, morphing into a new scene. Abby was no longer sitting in her office. She was now standing in front of a skyscraper in the middle of Philadelphia, a bank building. Mayhem.

At day's end, fifty-four people would be dead, including Bill. But he'd never know the death toll. He would never know about the child who had just left the dentist's office after having his braces taken off. He would never know about the pregnant executive, who had been crushed in the collapse, or the nation praying her baby would survive, prayers that were left unanswered. He would never know all of the lives affected by that single act. He would never know their pain. His pain ended the moment he pushed that button. But it was only the beginning of Abby's. She would come to know every single face, every single story.

"Why?" they asked. "If this man was in the care of a competent psychologist, why did this happen?"

Abby asked herself those same questions. She hid herself away in her apartment and tried to ignore her phone's incessant ringing. In the firestorm of a media circus that ensued, everyone wanted an interview with her - the woman who had reportedly told Bill it was "normal" for him to have fantasies of killing and mass destruction, post deployment. She had no clue as to how secured files and her treatment records were being leaked to the press.

Abby knew most of her colleagues would have treated Bill the same way she had, but they didn't come forward to support her. Instead, they crucified her publicly, anywhere they could find an outlet. She became the sacrificial lamb for America's pain, guilt and embarrassment, and she accepted the role as scapegoat. Abby believed she had failed that poor young soldier - a man who had been angry, confused and traumatized by the actions he, and others, had been forced to take. She believed she had given him permission to commit a horrendous act, an act which destroyed many lives. In his suicide note, Bill had said, "Perhaps society might be spared the impact of war if only the guilty suffered the consequences."

* * *

Abby awoke from the nightmare wild-eyed, covered in sweat. She was disoriented. Nothing looked familiar. *Where am I?* Her eyes darted around. She felt like she was hiding out, but this wasn't her apartment. *Where am I?* She sat up, clenching the sheets, trying to muffle her breathing while she listened for reporters. Her heart raced and she felt on edge. She felt panicked. *Breathe. Breathe!* Then it slowly dawned on her where she was. A sense of relief washed over her, followed by a sickening realization. *I can't do this anymore. I just can't.* Abby decided she could not go on like this, night after night. If she were to ever move on with her life, she needed to face her accusers, their hatred and their judgment. It made no sense she continue to hide out, to keep running. She made a decision: it was time for her to leave Winchester Bay.

* * *

Abby tucked her last cable knit sweater into her suitcase and sighed as she glanced around the small space. It had become home to her; she was not eager to leave it. A lot of what Craig said made sense. She needed to go back to Philadelphia, with her head held high, and confront the people who believed such terrible things about her.

She rationalized her leaving had nothing to do with Craig's confessing his feelings for her. But, just thinking about it, and the memory of his lips on hers, was enough to make her want to run away. It wasn't that she did not feel the same way about him. She did. She felt very strongly for him and believed she didn't deserve him. The therapist in her kept chiming in, warning her she was in no shape to commit in any way, and she agreed.

That made the decision to head back to Philadelphia a rather simple one. *Elementary, indeed*. Abby wouldn't have to face her feelings about Craig, and, if she were gone, he would realize he did not feel as strongly for her as he thought. *Yes, I'll go*. She smiled to herself, in satisfaction, confident she was right to leave. Zipping her suitcase shut, she opened the door of the cabin and stepped out. She closed her eyes, taking in a deep lung full of the cool morning air. *Boy, will I miss this place*. Breathing out slowly, she savored the moment, and slowly opened her eyes. Abby was about to step off of the boat when something caught her eye. She saw a shiny pink note taped to the cabin door. Abby smiled when she saw the childish squiggles. It was a note from Chloe.

Abby,

Please join us for a picnic at Umpqua Lighthouse at 4 o'clock.

It is a special picnic and you have to come. Please come.

Love,
Chloe

Abby stared at the note for a long moment, pondering what to do. The perfect spelling was almost as adorable as the abundance of hearts and flowers she had drawn in the margins. Clearly Chloe had put a great deal of effort into the missive.

She didn't think it was a good idea to encourage Chloe but, at the same time, she didn't have the heart to disappoint her. She hadn't purchased her ticket home yet, so she had some time. *What would it hurt to leave a few hours later?* Resolute she would still leave, she decided to go and enjoy the picnic. Craig deserved a "goodbye" and a "thank you" for all he had done for her. She wanted to be honest with him, and let him know it was not the right time for them to get involved in a serious relationship. *Yes... I'll tell him.*

Delighted with her decision, Abby put her suitcase back inside the cabin. She was excited at the idea of seeing Craig one last time and left the boat, walking in the direction of the lighthouse, south through several parks that were strung together buffering the shoreline from the highway that ran along the coast. She had been gazing at it for days, finding its simple beauty very alluring - the red, green and white colors contrasting with the midmorning sky. Since the picnic was scheduled for late afternoon, she had plenty of time to explore the area first. Abby hadn't had a chance to see the lighthouse up close.

As she was walking, a patrol car pulled up next to her. It was Paul, the sheriff who had given her his card after Craig spoke to him about protecting her. He drove slowly along the graveled park road, keeping pace with her steps. Taking the not-so-subtle hint, she turned to look at him.

"Everything alright today, Abby?" he asked. "Anyone giving you any trouble?"

Abby managed a smile and shook her head. "Everything's fine," she replied.

"Are you sure?" he asked, meeting her gaze pointedly. "I got word you were heading out."

"Word?" Abby asked suspiciously. She wondered how he could possibly know she planned to leave.

"Yes. When you notify the marina a boat will be vacant, they notify me. It's so I know which boats are empty and which are occupied," he calmly explained.

Abby nodded slowly as his words began to make sense to her. She had called the owner of the marina earlier that day to make sure her uncle's boat would be taken care of and maintained after she left.

"So, you *are* leaving?" His good nature meant she was willing to overlook how nosy he was being.

"Tonight," Abby confessed and grimaced when Paul's face grew serious.

"Did something happen to make you uncomfortable here?" he asked.

"No, not at all," Abby replied with a slow shake of her head. "I've decided it's time I face the people back home. The ones who think I have something to hide."

Paul chuckled as he leaned back in his seat. "I don't know, Abby. Seems to me, people like that shouldn't be worth your time, or a plane ticket." He shrugged and started the engine on the car. "Just so you know, you're always welcome here." He gave her a short wave and drove away.

Abby stared after him. His words struck her as she watched his car disappear down the road. *Maybe he is right. What do any of those people back in Philly matter to me, anyway?* The truth was Abby didn't like any of them. She had no interest in defending herself. *So why am I going back?* She was still absorbed in thought, contemplating it, when she reached the lighthouse.

* * *

» Chapter 10 «
~SERENADE~

Abby spent about an hour sitting at the edge of the water, watching the light waves ripple past, absorbing and internalizing the peace of her surroundings. Philadelphia was so much faster paced than Winchester Bay. When she first arrived, she thought the town to be quaint, strange and backwards. But now she reveled in its charm. It was nice to not feel pressured, not worry about traffic or care about the latest restaurant of choice. All of those things didn't really matter, especially when compared to water tickling her bare toes. She sighed contentedly, as she once again considered heading back to the boat. But the idea of not seeing Craig at least one last time, and not wanting to disappoint Chloe, kept her exactly where she was.

By the time she walked back to the lighthouse, it was a few minutes after four, the sun hanging much lower in the sky. Abby spotted a picnic table with a red-and-white checked tablecloth, and a large picnic basket with two wine glasses beside it. She thought it a little strange, as she didn't see anyone when she looked around. There was no sign of Craig or Chloe. *Where are they?* She sighed, then decided to sit down at the picnic table and wait.

Craig stepped out of the parking lot and walked around the side of the lighthouse. When he spotted Abby at the picnic table, his heart leaped into his throat and stayed there. He wondered what he should say to her, what she might say to him. He walked up behind her and spoke in his easy tone.

"Some picnic you've put together. Thank you!" He paused beside the table. Abby looked up at him with surprise, a hint of relief showing in her expression.

"What do you mean?" She was puzzled by his words. "Chloe invited me here. Didn't you put this picnic together?"

Before he had a chance to answer, music started playing from behind a tree, startling both of them. A violinist appeared from where he had obviously been hiding. When he stepped out from behind the tree, Craig recognized him right away as the music teacher from Chloe's school. Craig shook his head and wiped his hands across his face to try to hide his embarrassment. As the musician continued to play, Abby stood up from the picnic table, fascinated by his talent. It was amazing to hear such lovely music in an unexpected but beautiful setting.

Craig moved a little closer to her as they listened. When his fingers brushed the back of her hand, she did not pull hers away. Instead, she allowed him to intertwine their fingers. When the music stopped, the violinist bowed deeply, cast a wink in Craig's direction and then strolled off through the parking lot, as though serenading a surprise picnic was something he did every day. Craig wondered how many people were involved in setting this up. He was sure Paul had a hand in it.

"Oh, Abby," Craig said awkwardly, as he continued to hold her hand. "I think we've been set up."

Abby glanced at him, her own cheeks burning as she nodded slowly. "I think you're right."

Craig grimaced as he slipped his hand from hers. "I'm sorry. I'm sure you came for Chloe -"

"No," she said quickly and took his hand back into hers, closing both of her hands over his. "Craig, I came to talk to you, too. I need to tell you something." Her heart began to race as she wondered how he would react to the news she was leaving. A part of her wanted him to be fine with it, to understand. But a larger part of her wanted him to demand she stay. *How deep are his feelings?*

"I have some things I need to say to you, as well." Craig replied in a gentle but secretive tone. "Will you take a walk with me?"

"Sure." Abby nodded and tightened her grasp on his hand. She did not want to let him go, not just yet. Craig led her toward the lighthouse.

"Have you been up to the top yet?" he asked glancing her way.

"No," Abby shook her head. "I wasn't sure if it was open to the public

Craig smiled. His eyes flickered with delight. "Well, it isn't. But being a volunteer park ranger has its perks." He cleared his throat as he reached into his pocket and retrieved the key to the lighthouse door. "Actually, it only has one," he laughed, "and this is it." He pushed the door open and allowed Abby to step inside first. Abby led the way up the winding stairs. With each step she climbed, Craig's presence stirred her excitement. She felt like she was back in high school, sneaking off with a boy she had a crush on.

When they reached the top of the lighthouse, she was in awe. Her thoughts were silenced by the beauty of the view. She could barely take a breath.

The sky and the water merged to create such a beautiful horizon. Then she felt Craig's hands settle along her waist, sliding forward to wrap around her. She closed her eyes as a wave of warmth washed over her, and leaned back into him. She felt lovely in his arms, as if she was more beautiful reflected in his eyes.

"Craig, I need to say something-" Abby forced herself to begin a conversation very little of her wanted to have.

"No," he countered, knowing he might be pushing her too quickly, but willing to take the chance. "Please, let me tell you something first."

Abby agreed hesitantly, nodding as she turned to face him. The anxiety in his expression set her own nerves on edge, as she wondered what he had to say.

"Look, Abby, I know maybe the kiss at the dunes frightened you. But I... " he met her eyes. She hoped he might sweep in and kiss her again, but he continued to speak instead. "I need you to know I'm falling in love with you." He frowned when she cringed and glanced away. "I'm not trying to force you into anything," he assured her. "I want you to know-"

"I'm leaving tonight," she blurted out, before he could even finish his sentence.

"What?" He asked with surprise, taking a step back and releasing her from his arms.

"I think it's time I went back," she said nervously, staring hard at the wooden slats on the floor.

"Abby," Craig, at a loss, swept his hand through his hair. He wanted to tell her she couldn't go, that she had to stay, but he had no right.

"I think I need to face the past... you know... confront these people who are saying things about me—"

"Abby," he interrupted, struggling to meet her eyes, "are you telling me you don't have any feelings for me?" It was a bold question, but Craig had never shied from those.

Abby dropped her head while she bit into her bottom lip wishing she could avoid the awkward moment unfolding before her. She focused on her breathing, and then slowly raised her eyes to his. The moment her gaze met his, she was lost in it. How could she lie to him?

"Craig, I'm trying to tell you I'm not sure whether these feelings are fair," she said quietly.

"Fair?" he repeated as if he could not comprehend the use of the word. "Fair to whom?"

"To you," she replied softly.

"So, you think it is fair to take off without seeing this through, but not fair to admit how you really feel?" His voice raised an octave at the absurdity of the question. It made him think she did not have the same affection for him.

"It's not as simple as that," she protested and started to step past him. He grabbed her loosely around the waist, drawing her back toward him.

"Wait a minute. Just talk to me," he pleaded. He dreamed of the moment he would confess how he truly felt about her. He never imagined her responding by stating her intent was to go back to Philadelphia. "What isn't simple about it? You either have feelings for me, or you don't." Abby pushed away from him briefly.

"Craig... you lost your wife and survived it. You have a family, a community that loves you, a sweet, adorable, enchanting daughter, and you're stable. Me? I've gone through hell, still have nightmares, don't know what's left of my career, and can't bet on tomorrow. I haven't a clue what will happen from one minute to the next, or where my life's going. And *you* want a relationship with *me*? That's what is not fair, Craig. I'm a mess and the furthest thing from stable. Remember, I escaped the nut house. I can't make you any promises about today, let alone the future. I haven't a clue what it will hold."

Abby took a breath before plaintively asking, "Are you sure that's what you want? For Chloe?"

He tightened his grasp on her waist as he studied her with open adoration. "I'm not asking for promises," he said softly, his gaze melting into her eyes. "I'm just asking for a chance, and the truth." He smiled a little when he saw the blush rising in her cheeks. "Can you really tell me you don't feel the same way?"

Abby felt the heat rising in her cheeks and knew her blush had given her away. Closing her eyes, she took a breath of courage before trying once more, "Craig, I can't trust how I feel right now. It's all a jumble."

"Is it?" he inquired, and she felt his lips nearing hers. She didn't answer, and didn't open her eyes. She didn't dare breathe. She wanted only for him to cross the distance remaining between their lips and kiss her. His lips hovered so close, but they did not touch.

"Is it?" he asked again in a whisper.

"No," she replied, her voice trembling. She wanted so much to taste him. Her lips betrayed her, seeking his. The kiss which began subtly and sweetly became intensely passionate. Deeply passionate. She was lost in the moment and wanted more. Her mind, her body, her soul yearned to become one with Craig's. She melted into his being and her soul surrendered. As she was drifting into that dimension of sensory overload, the specter of fear reared its head and made her pull back.

"The picnic!" Abby reminded him breathlessly. It was not that she was hungry, or worried the food would spoil. Nor was she concerned Paul and Chloe's effort would go to waste. She needed to get away from his arms, wrapped so snugly around her. From the desire burning inside her. She was being drawn into something she had purposefully planned to avoid. Craig was coaxing her into admitting how deeply she had come to care for him, something she was not yet ready to declare.

* * *

"Oh... the picnic," he replied as he brushed her hair back over her shoulder. "Let's get back to it." He took her hand and led her back down the lighthouse stairs. He opened the door at the bottom, and they strolled across the grass towards the picnic table. The sun was very low in the sky, casting a soft glow across everything it touched, especially the water.

Abby could not believe how much the scenery had changed in so little time. Both in the bay, and in her heart. Never, in her wildest imagination, would she have believed taking her uncle's advice to come to Winchester Bay would forever alter her path.

Craig poured them both a glass of wine as she got comfortable at the picnic table. He offered her a glass and held up his own.

"To us," he said and took a long swallow. Abby took a sip of her wine and smiled as he sat down beside her. The picnic basket included peanut butter and jelly sandwiches, and cookies.

"I guess she thought the ice cream would melt," he laughed and shook his head.

"She was right." Abby grinned and took another sip of her wine. Her mind was still whirling with everything that was happening. She had no idea whether she should change her mind about leaving. It was clear Craig believed his feelings were genuine. She kept telling herself she should know better.

As they ate, they talked about Paul and Chloe, and how sweet it was they had done this for them.

"She really likes you," Craig reminded Abby. Abby smiled and gazed out across the water. Her profile framed by the setting sun was too beautiful for Craig to resist. He reached up and lightly caressed her cheek, his fingertips tickling the side of her neck.

Abby's laughter filled the air as they shared the last glass of wine. To Craig, the way her eyes sparkled was intoxicating. He suddenly grew serious, and reached for her hand. Her laughter faded, leaving only the sound of water gently breaking against sand.

"What is it?" she asked. Craig stood, drawing her up as well. He led her to the small fence which separated the lighthouse from the water. After beholding the setting sun a few long heartbeats, he turned to look directly at Abby.

"Are you going to run away from this?" His voice was thick with emotion. He locked eyes with her and Abby cringed inwardly. It was the moment she had hoped to avoid. Craig could see straight into her. It was something she had never experienced with a man before. She had to make a choice. Should she lie or be honest with him?

"Craig," she beseeched softly and looked away.

"No, Abby," Craig said firmly though his tone was still quiet. He gently cupped her cheek, guiding her eyes back to his. "Just tell me the truth, before I get in further than I already have. Are you going to run away from me?"

Abby's eyes closed against his probing stare. She wanted nothing more than to fall into his arms and confess her deepest feelings, but she was afraid. She was afraid she was wrong, just as she had been with Bill. She had followed her instincts then, allowing her emotions to guide her. The end result was destruction and pain. She couldn't trust herself, couldn't risk being wrong again. Her heart pounded.

Craig trailed his thumb along the curve of her cheek as he waited patiently for her answer. She could feel the heat of his lips drawing closer to hers, knowing in the next moment, he would be kissing her. The sensation was hypnotic and inviting. She wanted to savor it, to draw it in close. Her loins burned. She wanted him deeply but felt she shouldn't. Suddenly she pulled back, her eyes open, turning her head slightly to avoid the impending kiss. Her breath was shallow and she dared not allow him to continue, or she would never get on the plane.

"It's okay," he said, as he let his hand fall away from her cheek. "Maybe it was me getting my hopes up. Maybe, it was me imagining you felt the same way I did." He was disappointed. When she glanced up at him, he turned to face the water below. Abby felt the absence of his touch with an ache and a longing, as if a part of her had been ripped away. She had never experienced such intense hunger for anyone. Her life was entirely focused on the emotional needs of others. She had never been concerned with her own needs. Hadn't even been aware she had any.

One of her friends had once beamed about how wonderful it was to be in love. Abby couldn't relate. At the time, she joked about love being all neurotransmitters and hormones. But now she knew that was not the case. She had come to an epiphany while in Winchester Bay: she found what was really important in life. She was connected to community, to Craig and Chloe, and to a primal element that didn't exist in Philadelphia. Abby had found acceptance here, and awakened a side of her she'd never nourished.

Love. It seemed so simple now. She loved this place and, as that love grew in her like a seed, she was able to share it with others. She now knew love personally, how it could slip inside of you and possess every fiber of your being, leaving you very few options. In the loss of their connection, Abby realized she had grown to love Craig, and this was her chance. She could not allow fear to keep her from him. She had met the man of her girlhood dreams and wanted to savor every moment she had with him.

"Craig?" she said. But this time, it was he who refused to look at her. He feared she was going to Dear John him, giving him the "it's not you, it's me" speech. That would crush him. Instead, she cupped his cheeks in the palms of her hands, following his example and turning his face toward hers. "I'm not going anywhere," she said.

She leaned forward in the same moment he did. Their kiss was full of all of the fear and joy they felt. A heady mixture of elation, terror and desperation.

Neither of them knew exactly what to expect, but both of them were certain of one thing: it was a new beginning. Together they would make a fresh start, replacing the heartache and tragedies of the past with something lighter, something brighter, something full of love and something worth all the risk.

* * *

Other Works by Emily Porterfield

DINNER FOR TWO – Lucy is an elegant, snobby, food critic. Her palate is the most sophisticated, and the most unforgiving. Everyone wants their food to pass her approval. But not Russ. He's the new sensation on the block, the farthest thing from refined… but oh, can he cook! Their attraction is electrifying but they are as different as night and day. Can they bridge the gap to make it work? This light-hearted romantic comedy packs loads of fun.

RETURN TO MISTY FALLS – It's been six years since Rae's been home. Six years in the city, focused on her career. But when news reaches her that her parents are losing their homestead, all she can think of is what she stands to lose – the dream of being married on that land. Rae returns home with selfish motives: she wants to salvage her dream and… perchance have one last

fling before she ties the knot. She returns home curious about the boy she left behind. But little does she know, he has been waiting for her. He never gave his heart to anyone else…
Coming in February 2014.

You can find Emily's books on Amazon at:

http://www.amazon.com/author/emilyporterfield

About the Author

Emily Porterfield has been writing for most of her life. She started in her early teens, writing primarily prose, poetry, lyrics and music. She was first published in college - publishing multiple pieces every year – and added nonfiction writing in graduate school. Emily is a composer, explorer, nature photographer and amateur filmmaker. You'll usually find her living off the beaten path enjoying many a Norman Rockwell moments. She loves roaring fires, quiet moments at home, and a good German Riesling. When she isn't stargazing, hanging out at the farmer's market, hugging trees or mastering a Rachmaninov piece, you'll find her writing sweet romances with a bit of comedy, suspense or drama, in bite-sized novella and cozy novel formats.

Join Emily's mailing list at her website, EMILYPORTERFIELD.COM, for giveaways, pre-release discounts, reveals and more. You can also find her on Facebook. Stop by and say, "Hi." https://www.facebook.com/emilyporterfieldbooks